The Librarian
from the
Black Lagoon

by Mike Thaler · pictures by Jared Lee

SCHOLASTIC INC.
New York Toronto London Auckland Sydney

For Jared D. Lee,

Friend, partner, genius

—M.T.

To the nice people who work at the

Public Library in Lebanon, Ohio

—J.L.

Library of Congress Catalog Card Number: 96-70646

ISBN 0-590-50311-1

Text copyright © 1997 by Mike Thaler.
Illustrations copyright © 1997 by Jared D. Lee Studio, Inc.
All rights reserved. Published by Scholastic Inc.

10 9 8 7 6 5 4 3 2 1

Printed in the U.S.A.   24

First printing, August 1997

Today our class is going to the library.

We've been hearing some really scary things about the place.

The library is somewhere behind the boiler room.
It's called "MEDIA CENTER OF THE EARTH."

Mrs. Beamster is the librarian.
The kids call her "THE LAMINATOR."

They say she laminates you if you talk in the library.

She also has a library assistant named IGOR.

You know you're getting close to the library
by the signs on the wall.

They say you're allowed to stay in the library as long as
you can hold your breath.
Some kids last as long as a minute.

That doesn't include the time in
the *DECONTAMINATION ROOM.*

There you put on hair nets and rubber gloves.

Next, you have to go through the *GUM DETECTOR!*

Once you're finally in the library, you can't
actually check out books.
In fact, you can't take them off the shelves.
To keep the books in alphabetical order,
Mrs. Beamster bolts them together.

Also, they say, the shelves are electrified.

If you twist your neck and squint,
you can read the spines.

Everyone says the best part of a library visit is *STORYTIME*. All the kids stand at attention while Mrs. Beamster reads one of the cards from the card catalog.

Or, if you catch her in a good mood, she'll recite the Dewey decimal system by heart.

They say Mrs. Beamster has a crush on Mr. Dewey and that
she carries his picture in a lead locket around her neck.

She also has rubber stamps on the soles of her shoes.
And, wherever she steps . . . it says *OVERDUE!*

She seems to have ears on the back of her head.

If she catches you whispering . . .

YOU'RE *LAMINATED!*

They say she puts glue on all the chairs
so you won't *WRIGGLE*.

Then she shows you slides of all her vacations since 1902.
She goes to the same place every year – the Library of Congress.

Mrs. Beamster also subscribes to three magazines:
The Morticians Monthly, *The Complete Pamphlet of Zip Codes*,
and *Spots Illustrated: The Magazine for Cleaner Laundry*.
These you *DO* get to read.

But stay away from her plants. They are VENUS FLY TRAPS!

And don't pet the animals in her petting zoo, which contains a PIRANHA and a PORCUPINE.

Don't go near her computer either, it uses a *real* MOUSE!

Well, it's time to go.

As we get near the library there *are* lots of signs.

We march right in and sit down in little chairs.
These must be the ones without glue.
Mrs. Beamster comes over with an armful of books
and puts them on our table.

Then she smiles and hands me one.
It's a book of KNOCK-KNOCK JOKES!

I'm going to love the library!